THE OLD TIRED GIVING TREE
© Copyright 1999 by ARO Publishing.
All rights reserved, including the right of reproduction in whole or in part in any form. Designed and produced by ARO Publishing.
Printed in the U.S.A. P.O. Box 193 Provo, Utah 84603

ISBN 0-89868-443-9–Library Bound
ISBN 0-89868-444-1–Soft Bound
ISBN 0-89868-445-5-Trade

**WALKER MEMORIAL LIBRARY
800 MAIN STREET
WESTBROOK, ME 04092
(207) 854-0630**

A PREDICTABLE WORD BOOK

THE OLD TIRED GIVING TREE

Story by Janie Spaht Gill, Ph.D.
Illustrations by Bob Reese

ARO PUBLISHING

In the middle of a field,
there stood an old, worn out tree.

It looked very tired and ordinary
as can be.

An owl and his family
spied a hole inside the tree.

The owl said, "Let's stop here.
We are tired and need some sleep."

A woodpecker flying by,
spied the bark upon the tree.

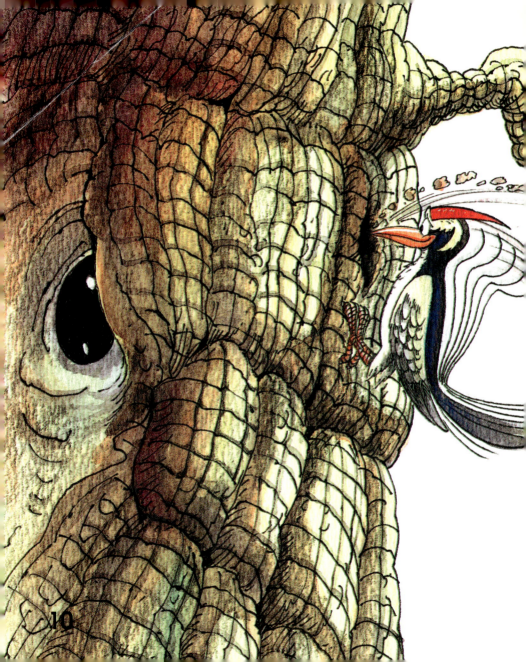

He said, "I will peck it here, and make a home for me."

A boy playing in the field,

saw the branches of the tree.

The boy said, "With nails and wood,

I'll build a treehouse in this tree."

A man passing by,
saw the twigs upon the tree.

The man said, "I will cut those twigs and build a fire for me."

Mother Nature had been watching and you could tell that she was pleased.

She said, "You are generous and kind, and a truly giving tree.

I want the world to see
you are not an ordinary tree.

Because you look so old and tired,
I will give you these new leaves."

JUV
PIC
Gill